Hey Jack!

Hey Jack! Books

First American Edition 2020
Kane Miller, A Division of EDC Publishing
Original Title: Hey Jack: The Extra-Special Group
Text Copyright © 2015 Sally Rippin
Illustration Copyright © 2015 Stephanie Spartels
Logo and Design Copyright © 2015 Hardie Grant Egmont
First published in Australia by Hardie Grant Egmont

For information contact:
Kane Miller, A Division of EDC Publishing
P.O. Box 470663
Tulsa, OK 74147-0663
www.kanemiller.com
www.edcpub.com
www.usbornebooksandmore.com

Library of Congress Control Number: 2019951181

Printed and bound in the United States of America
1 2 3 4 5 6 7 8 9 10
ISBN: 978-1-68464-133-8

Hey Jack!

The Extra-special Group

By Sally Rippin

Illustrated by Stephanie Spartels

Kane Miller
A DIVISION OF EDC PUBLISHING

Chapter One

This is Jack. Today Jack is feeling stuck. His class is doing a spelling test and he can't remember how to spell any of the words.

Jack is good at art.

He is good at soccer.

He is even pretty good
at math, but he is terrible
at spelling.

No matter how hard he
stares at the words, they
just won't stay in his brain.

A big salty tear slides
down Jack's nose and
drops onto his paper.

He quickly rubs his eyes before anyone sees. It's no use! The harder he tries, the worse it is.

Finally the bell goes.

At last! Jack thinks.
He breathes out a big
hot puff of air.

"OK, class," Ms. Walton
says. "Put your tests on
my desk before you go
out to play."

Jack folds his paper in
half so no one can see his
terrible work.

4

He drops it on Ms. Walton's desk. Then he runs into the hallway to get his snack from his bag. Already Jack's heart feels lighter.

But then he hears Ms. Walton's voice. "Jack, can you come back in here for a moment?"

Jack's heart squeezes into a ball. Billie looks at him with a worried face.

"I'll wait for you," she whispers.

"Thanks, Billie," Jack

says. He trudges back into the classroom.

"Did you try your hardest on this test, Jack?" Ms. Walton asks him.

Jack nods. His eyes begin to fill with tears again. "I can't do it," he whispers. "I'm just no good at spelling. Or reading."

"Oh dear. I can see how hard this is for you, Jack. I think it might be time for you to get a bit of extra help from Miss Campbell," Ms. Walton says.

Jack gasps. "But then everyone will know how bad I am!"

8

"Oh, Jack!" Ms. Walton says. "There's nothing wrong with needing a little extra help with some subjects. You are very clever. But not everyone learns at the same speed. I'll see if Miss Campbell can fit you in tomorrow after recess."

10

"But that's when we have art," Jack says sadly.

"Sorry, Jack," Ms. Walton says. "But I think it is important that we help you catch up to the rest of the class. You want to be able to read what your friends are reading, don't you?"

11

Jack nods slowly. Billie and his other friends are reading cool books. He is still reading books for babies.

But Miss Campbell's extra classes? What will he tell his friends? They will all know how bad he is at spelling if he goes to see Miss Campbell!

"Jack," Ms. Walton says kindly, "sometimes these things turn out better than you think they will."

Jack sighs as he plods back out of the classroom. Billie is waiting for him in the hallway.

"What did Ms. Walton want?" she asks.

"Nothing," Jack says. Even though Billie is his best friend, he still feels too embarrassed to tell her the truth.

Chapter Two

The next day after recess, Billie heads to the art room. Jack starts walking towards Miss Campbell's room instead.

"Where are you going?"
Billie asks Jack. "Aren't
you coming to art?"

Jack shakes his head.
"I'm going to the nurse,"
he says quietly. "I don't
feel very well."

This isn't a complete lie.
Jack *does* feel funny in his
tummy.

But he doesn't like lying to his best friend. And he is sure the extra classes are going to be boring. Or hard. Or probably both. These thoughts muddle up his tummy and make him feel terrible.

"Do you want me to come?" Billie asks.

Jack shakes his head. "No.
I just need to lie down
for a little bit, I think."

Jack walks down the long hallway. He stops in front of Miss Campbell's door.

Jack has never been into this room before. He tries to imagine what it looks like. He takes a deep breath and knocks on the door.

Miss Campbell opens the
door. She smiles widely.
"Hello, Jack! Come in."

Jack steps inside. In the middle of the room there is a big round table. Some kids are sitting at the table doing puzzles. Along the back wall is a row of computers. One of the kids at a computer turns around and waves at him. "Hey, Jack!"

Jack is surprised. "Aaron?"

Aaron is in the classroom next to Jack's. Everybody likes him.

Jack didn't think Aaron would need extra help.

"Why don't you take the computer next to Aaron's?" Miss Campbell says. "He can show you the frog game." She sits down to help one of the kids at the table.

"Game?" Jack says as he sits next to Aaron. "We get to play games here?"

"Well, it's work, really,"
Aaron says. "See, when
you get the word right,
the frog jumps across the
pond. It's hard at first.
But now I'm up to level
seventeen."

Aaron sets up the game
and Jack tests it out. At
first he can't make the
frog jump at all.

But soon he gets better at spelling the words right.

"Hey look, Aaron!" Jack says excitedly. "I'm already up to the next level!"

"Cool!" says Aaron. "You're much quicker than me. It took me two days to get past the first level."

Jack smiles proudly. *Maybe I'm not bad at spelling after all*, he thinks.

Chapter Three

"How are you doing
with the frogs, Jack?" Miss
Campbell says. She pulls
up a chair to sit next
to him.

"Good, I think," says Jack shyly. "Do you want me to start work now?"

"This *is* work, Jack!" Miss Campbell laughs. "These games will help your spelling and reading."

Jack grins.

"Sometimes when you come here we'll work together at my desk," Miss Campbell explains. "Other times you will practice on these computer games, or work with the word puzzles. I think you will improve very quickly.

Look how fast you've learned this one!"

Miss Campbell looks around the room and claps her hands. "OK, my extra-special group!" she calls. "Time to go back to your classes."

She turns back to Jack. "You've done well today.

Would you like to come back next week?"

"Yes, please!" says Jack.

Jack says goodbye to Aaron. Then he runs down the hallway to join his class in the art room.

Billie waves and pats the stool next to her where she has saved a spot for him.

Suddenly Jack feels bad. He wishes he hadn't lied to Billie. They usually tell each other everything.

"Billie," he whispers. "I wasn't really at the nurse."

"I know," Billie whispers back. "I saw you go into Miss Campbell's room."

"Really?" Jack feels his face burn hot. "So then you know I was …"

"Getting extra help." Billie nods. Then she frowns at Jack. "It hurt my feelings when I found out you lied to me."

Jack hangs his head. "I'm sorry," he says in a quiet voice. "I thought you'd think I wasn't smart."

"Jack!" Billie says. "Did you really think that? Don't you remember how bad I was at ballet? And swimming? And you never thought I wasn't smart, did you?"

"Of course not!" Jack says.

"Nobody can be good at everything," Billie says.

"Jack, you are good at
lots of things. In fact,
you are great at the most
important thing."

"What's that?" Jack asks.

"Being a best friend." Billie smiles.

Jack grins. "Thanks. I'm glad we're still friends."

"*Best* friends," Billie says. "But that means telling the truth, OK? Always."

"OK!" says Jack. He feels very happy. Ms. Walton was right.

Sometimes things turn out *much* better than Jack thinks they will.

Hey Jack! **The Crazy Cousins** By Sally Rippin

Hey Jack! **The Scary Solo** By Sally Rippin

Hey Jack! **The Winning Goal** By Sally Rippin

Hey Jack! **The Robot Blues** By Sally Rippin

Hey Jack! **The Worry Monsters** By Sally Rippin

Hey Jack! **The New Friend** By Sally Rippin

Hey Jack! **The Worst Sleepover** By Sally Rippin

Hey Jack! **The Circus Lesson** By Sally Rippin

Hey Jack! **The Bumpy Ride** By Sally Rippin

Hey Jack! **The Top Team** By Sally Rippin

Hey Jack! **The Playground Problem** By Sally Rippin

Hey Jack! **The Best Party Ever** By Sally Rippin

Hey Jack! **The Bravest Kid** By Sally Rippin

Hey Jack! **The Big Adventure** By Sally Rippin

Hey Jack! **The Toy Sale** By Sally Rippin

Hey Jack! **The Star of the Week** By Sally Rippin

Hey Jack! **The Extra-special Group** By Sally Rippin

Billie B. Brown & Hey Jack! **The Book Buddies** by Sally Rippin

Read them all!
Including a new title
starring both Jack AND Billie